Table of Contents

The Ten Plagues of Egypt.....................8

Attributions

Evocation

Then the magicians said to Pharaoh,
"This is the finger of God."
But Pharaoh's heart was hardened,
and he would not listen to them,
as the Lord had said.

Exodus 8:19

Foreword

The book of Exodus was written by the statesman / general / prophet Moses to narrate the departure of the Israelite tribes from Egypt. Exodus describes how God called Moses to lead the Exodus, telling Moses to confront Pharaoh himself with His demands at the royal court.

Moses obeyed, and delivered Yahweh's demands to Pharaoh. Pharaoh demurred. The Israelites provided free labour to the Egyptian state and Pharaoh had no intention of letting it walk off the job without a fight. Pharaoh instructed his military police accordingly and had Moses cast out of his presence.

Moses, for his part, was not going to take "no" for an answer. He confronted the royal court again the next day beside the river Nile, crying aloud to Yahweh that its waters be turned into blood. Yahweh did so.

The Egyptians – apart from Pharaoh, who remained obdurate - began taking Moses seriously. In Egyptian eyes, Moses was clearly a magician of exceptional power: who soon gave additional demonstrations that his abilities far outstripped those of the royal magicians at court.

From that time forth, Moses entered to speak at Pharaoh's court whenever he wished. The Egyptians feared this man – and with good reason. Anyone who could turn the Nile waters into blood could very easily ruin the entire land of Egypt, or kill thousands at a word. And that, over the subsequent nine plages, is precisely what happened.

Today's readers, confronted with this synopsis of the Exodus story, are immediately confronted with various difficulties. We are so far removed from the worldview of the ancient Egyptians that the emotional impact of Exodus completely bypasses us.

For the Egyptians in Pharaoh's time did not just vaguely acknowledge the existence of their gods, like nominal believers do in our own day. The ancient Egyptians lived every hour of every day believing their gods were nearby and intimately involved in every aspect of their lives.

Each day Khepri propelled the sun through the sky overhead. Ra, the sun-god, was incarnate in the Pharaoh himself. When they were in good health, they sacrificed in gratitude to Isis. Whenever someone fell sick, they beseeched Imhotep to heal them. Sacrifices to Hapi ensured the Nile would flood and water their crops. Prayers to Neper and Nepri were repaid with good harvests. The rites paid to Hathor prospered their herds of livestock. Additional sacrifices to Geb increased the fertility of the soil, and to Khnum protected the Nile source from contamination.

Knowing these things might help the reader more readily appreciate just what it was that Moses was accomplishing in the Exodus. Moses was not just some simple spokesman for an obscure Israelite deity badgering an uninterested monarch. Moses was an ambassador from Yahweh, whose credentials was trumpeted by awesome displays of divine power: Moses announced plague after plague to devastate the entire land of Egypt, demonstrating that his God held the very lives of the Egyptians in His hand.

In other words, Moses – as the mouth of Yahweh – was challenging the entire Egyptian pantheon to prove its might against the undeniable power of his God. Can Khnum protect the Nile from Yahweh's curse? Or Hathor the livestock? Or Nepri the grain? Or Ra the sunlight? Why are the gods of Egypt struck dumb? Why can't the gods of Egypt protect their votaries?

Hopefully, this short introduction explains why the poems in this collection are cast in the form of a series of duels of power between Yahweh and the Egyptian gods. Indeed, this is certainly how contemporary Egyptians and Israelites would have understood the ten plagues and their resulting aftermath.

Readers interested in reading more original poetry are invited to connect with me via the social media links provided at my website: antipodeanwriter.wordpress.com.

Antipodean Writer
September 2020

Preface

This work is a series of ten poems exploring and celebrating the victory of Yahweh over the Egyptian pantheon, as related in the Book of Exodus.

According to Exodus, Yahweh brought ten plagues to sequentially afflict the land of Egypt.

1. Turning the Nile to blood.

2. Plague of frogs.

3. Plague of gnats / lice.

4. Plague of flies.

5. Death of livestock.

6. Plague of boils.

7. Violent hailstorm.

8. Plague of locusts.

9. Darkness.

10. Death of firstborn.

Each poem in this work describes one of the ten plagues listed above. Relevant Egyptian gods and their functions are also noted in the introductions to each poem as an aid to the reader.

Readers who enjoy original poetry are invited to check out my other poetry collections.

Poetry Collections by Antipodean Writer

- Ancient Greek Heroes
- Angels, Spirits & Dreams of Men
- Antonym Poetry
- Arthurian Legends
- Bible Heroes
- Orpheus Sings
- The Road to Hell
- Songs of the Dwarves
- Sonnet Collections
- Tales from the Forgotten Isles
- Ten Plagues of Egypt

Antipodean Writer
September 2020

The Ten Plagues of Egypt

Yahweh versus the Egyptian Pantheon

Plague One: Waters turned to blood

First Yahweh struck the gods of Nile

As He their waters did defile

And turned to blood. What could god Khnum

Do to prevent it? Mute and dumb

And helpless, Egypt's god is proved.

Are Hapi or Osiris moved

Their own devotees to protect

As all Egyptians might expect?

Like Hapi, god Osiris fails -

For Yahweh's supreme might prevails!

Moses spoke, then Aaron's staff

Gave Egypt only blood to quaff:

Each river, each canal and pond

Are turned to blood, here and beyond,

Throughout all Egypt. Each vessel

Of drinking water starts to smell,

Is turned undrinkable. All fish

Turn belly up. The people wish

To find fresh water, so dug they

That week, sinking wells every day.

The Nile stank, its smell arose

To nauseate the royal nose

And all his court. Still Pharaoh barred

His heart to God, remaining hard

And obdurate as flint or rock.

His magicians also took stock

Of Moses' powers. By some trick

They duplicate Moses' magic

(Although on a much smaller scale

Then those of Moses do entail).

So Pharaoh, duly unimpressed,

Dismissed Moses as alchemist

Despite the Nile running slow

And sluggish as cold blood does flow,

Congealing with stinking pisces,

Whose taint far-mingles with the seas.

Plague Two: Frogs

Egyptian Pantheon

Heqt was the goddess of fertility and had the head of frog.

Next Yahweh struck goddess Heket

With powers that He restrained yet

Lest Egypt be wholly destroyed.

A myriad frogs Yahweh employed

In countless millions on the land

To come when Aaron stretched his hand

On Egypt's waters. Next the plague

Of frogs emerge which quickly made

Their lives a misery: each room

Was filled with frogs! On oven, loom,

On bed or table they would hop -

Unending hordes that do not stop!

Heket is useless! Cannot she

Stop this frog plague? All entreaty

Is vain! In anger does Pharaoh

Summon magicians. Can also

They do this thing? They can. They do:

They summon frogs, and this they shew

To Pharaoh, who dismissed the art

Of Moses with new-hardened heart.

Can their magic make disappear

This plague of frogs, who fill the ear

With croaks? Nor magic, nor Heket,

Alas! Pharaoh is forced to get

Moses and Aaron to Yahweh

To intercede and for him pray!

They pray. That instant, all frogs die!

Heket again does nothing. Why?

Yahweh all Egypt with frogs fills

In plague proportions, then He kills

Them all. All Egypt gathered heaps

Of frogs together, and up seeps

The stench of dead-frogs piled high

Up everywhere just where they lie.

All Egypt sighs with huge relief -

The frogs are gone! But their belief

In Heket shatters. Deaf and dumb

Is Heket's aid when frog-plagues come.

Plague Three: Gnats

Then Yahweh struck Geb to the dust!

How much longer could Egypt trust

A god which proved so powerless

Against Yahweh? To the distress

Of Egypt, Aaron stretches out

His staff. Immediately, all about

From out the dust spring plagues of lice

And gnats, that cover in a trice

All men and beasts, all cloth and skin.

King Pharaoh calls his sorcerers in

Demanding whether also they

Can create lice? To his dismay

They could not. "Pharaoh, mighty King,

The Finger of God does this thing!"

Defeated, the wizards withdraw,

For Pharaoh's anger, as before,

Rises against the God Yahweh.

Why does not Geb Pharaoh obey?

Where is Geb's earth-suffused power?

It seems Egyptian gods all cower

Before Yahweh, nor can oppose

God Yahweh's will. Still, Pharaoh knows

Egyptian gods may yet prevail.

How can the gods of Egypt fail?

The years have numbered some thousands

Since Egypt rose upon the sands

To glory with her pantheon

Of gods. Yahweh has not yet won.

Plague Four: Flies

Egyptian Pantheon

Khepri was the god os sunrise and sunset and had the head of a scarab.

Then Yahweh struck down god Khepri,

Lord of the flies, who claimed that he

Moved the day-sun across the skies

Until its setting. Yet are flies

Raised in their millions at the sound

Of Moses' voice, covering the ground

Of the Egyptians. The Hebrews

In Goshen, this plague calmly views:

For not one insect, not one fly

Plagues Goshen, though it is hard by

The lands where the Egyptians dwell.

Does Khepri care not that there fell

Flies to plague Egypt, millions strong?

What have the Egyptians done wrong?

Are their gods weak? Or perhaps they

Are powerless against Yahweh?

Khepri is silent. Pharaoh pleads

With Moses that what Egypt needs

Is freedom from this insect crowd

Invading all their homes. Aloud

He begs that Yahweh take the flies

Away, as Khepri aid denies.

So Moses heard. Then Moses prayed.

His intercession duly made,

The flies vanish, even as though

There were a nightmare phantom. So

Pharaoh decides that He is sure

Past agreements he can abjure.

The flies are gone! He power craves,

And power requires Hebrew slaves!

So Yahweh then the next plague sends

To thwart Pharaoh, to gain His ends.

Plague Five: Death of livestock

Then Yahweh struck goddess Hathor

As one by one he declares war

Against false gods, showing them weak:

Too feeble to aid those who seek

Their favour. Hathor over herds

Had care, till Yahweh spoke these words:

That all the herds of Egypt will

Be struck with plagues, and falling ill

Shall die: the horse and the donkey,

Camel, and cow, and goat shall be

Afflicted. But Hebrew livestock

Will not be harmed. Then, as the shock

Sinks in: Egyptian animals die

And in their rigor mortis lie.

Aghast, the men of Egypt see

Their livestock perish miserably

Before their eyes! Hathor, appear

And heal our cattle! Desperate fear

Grows rampant as Hathor does not.

Hathor, apparently, forgot

Her people, as her beasts in death

Lie motionless, devoid of breath,

To blacken in the scorching sun.

And Yahweh's plagues have just begun.

Plague Six: Boils

Isis was the goddess of health (amongst other things).
Imhotep was the god of healing.

Then Yahweh struck Isis, goddess

Of health and healing. None-the-less

Pharaoh refused to trust Yahweh

Over Egyptian gods had sway.

Moses took soot in his two hands

From out a kiln, and as he stands

Before Pharaoh, that dust he threw:

And over all Egypt it blew

Becoming boils! Hot and sore

Upon the skin they sprung and bore

Dull-itching scabs, and pus weeping,

And broken skin with blood seeping

Over man and beast. Isis! Come heal!

Egyptians pray, daily appeal

For Isis' intervention. They

Beseech her healing every day!

No healing comes, just prolonged pain.

What reasons can these plagues explain?

The Hebrews remain healthy, hale,

While all the Egyptians bewail

Their burning sores and bleeding skin:

While Isis and her divine kin

Do nothing! Prayers to empty air

Are made to gods that are not there.

Plague Seven: Hail

Egyptian Pantheon

Nut was the goddess of the sky.
Shu was the god of wind and air.

Next Yahweh struck the goddess Nut

Who claimed she could the heavens shut

Or open. Yahweh struck at Shu -

Nut's father – at the same time too:

For Yahweh promised pouring hail

Upon all Egypt, to unveil

His mighty power as supreme

Over Egyptian gods who deem

That they are gods, but gods are not:

Merely a weak, impotent lot.

Moses, his hand, does upwards raise:

Large hailstones flatten all the maize

And growing shoots, the standing crop.

Then as the heavy hailstones drop -

Strange fires flashed continually

Amidst the hail incessantly.

Skulls shattered, and men's bones did break

For those who shelter did forsake

Despite the warning Moses gave

To the Egyptians who would save
Their lives by staying within doors
Cowering in safety, as downpours
Of hailstones fall in deadly spate.
Why does their god Shu hesitate
To stop the hail? Why Nut, O why
Does not she shut the angry sky
And cease the hailstorm deluge? For
More hailstones ceaselessly downpour
As all without are battered dead:
Their broken, beaten bodies bled
Upon the ground. Yet in Goshen,
Dwell there in safety Hebrew men:
No hailstones rained. Then Pharaoh's pleas
Become urgent as the king sees
Egypt is ruined and starve may:
Unless Moses entreats Yahweh.
Moses entreats. Yahweh concludes
The hailstorm, which Egypt denudes
Of all its young barley and flax
Crushed by the hail like frail wax
Melted when thrust into the fire.
Pharaoh waxes in his ire
And turns his heart as hard as ice
And heeds only his own advice.

Plague Eight: Locusts

Egyptian Pantheon

Neper was the god of grain.
Nepri was the goddess of grain.
Set was the god of disorder.

Then Yahweh struck the gods of grain -

Neper and Nepri – as again

Moses his hand to heaven raised.

Then Pharaoh apprehensive gazed

As clouds of locusts filled the skies.

All Egypt saw with daunted eyes,

And looked stark ruin in the face

As greenery, without a trace

Did vanish. The locusts devour

Every green thing: shoot, tree and bower

They demolish as against Set's

Untamed disorder Yahweh lets

Egypt see His superior might

When Moses, praying in the sight

Of Pharaoh, asks Yahweh to free

Egypt from locusts. Instantly

Yahweh a strong wind from the west

Caught up and drove every locust

Into the Red Sea where they drowned.

Instead of chaos, Egypt found

Order imposed. What did Set do?

Nothing, of course. The wind which blew

From Yahweh ends the locusts' sway

As the insects are blown away.

Thus Set is humbled and restrained

By Yahweh: all his power constrained!

Whether enraged, or sunk in grief:

Set must acknowledge as his chief

Yahweh. Not Pharaoh – who aspires

To keep the Hebrews. He retires

With hardened heart and mind unbent.

So Yahweh the next plague on him sent.

Plague Nine: Darkness

Egyptian Pantheon

Ra was the god of the sun.

Now Egypt's greatest god is Ra

That all Egyptians near and far

Worship: the sun-god, whose light-shine

Banishes night. He is divine!

For without Ra there is no day,

The sun will fail and flee away.

Therefore god Ra does Yahweh smite

And takes from Egypt her sunlight.

When Moses' stretches out his hand

To heaven, there falls on the land

A thick darkness, that can be felt -

For three whole days! The people knelt

And cried to Ra! What could Ra do

Against the God of gods? They sue

For Ra's protection. Dark prevails,

And all Egypt in terror quails.

Yahweh trumped Ra and quenched the sun!

The facts were plain, for everyone

Saw that the Hebrews still had light

Over Goshen. What god could fight

Such overwhelming power? They cry

To Pharaoh that they should not die!

Ra is proved helpless, as are they!

As you love life – send them away!

Pharaoh despised the Hebrew's God:

And wielding an iron rod

Prevents the Hebrews to depart

Egypt, hardening his adamant heart.

"Go Moses! Never see my face

Again, or you shall die!" (The race

Of Hebrews must remain my slaves -

So Pharaoh thought.) But Moses braves

The rage of Pharaoh. "As you say -

You shall not see me from today."

Moses turns upon his heel

And leaves. But the Egyptians feel

Great trepidations, growing fright:

As their days are engulfed by night.

Plague Ten: Death of firstborn

Egyptian Pantheon
Pharaoh was believed to be the sun-god, Ra, incarnate.

What god of Egypt can resist

Yahweh who has their powers dismissed?

Their potency, their vaunted names

Are shown up false. Yahweh proclaims

He has outshone and overmastered

All Egypt's gods who have been blasted

By His plagues. They could do naught

To oppose Him. For as they fought

They were thrown down, for Yahweh did

All that He wished. All that He bid

He has accomplished as a fact:

Egypt hardly remains intact

With its false idols, carved in stone,

Served by their priests: are helpless shown!

Gods unable to perform deeds

No matter what the desperate needs

Of Egypt are. The gods are dead!

Destruction upon Egypt's head

Descends: Yahweh strikes the firstborn

Of Egypt. From this life is torn
The firstborn child of every slave -
Now hurried to a lifeless grave.
The firstborn of each Egypt priest,
Each farmer, fisherman, has ceased
To breath. The firstborn of the king -
Of Pharaoh, too, has stopped living:
His corpse is cold. Ear-piercing wails
Are heard as loud mourning assails
The ears of Pharaoh. "We are dead
If the slave-Hebrews are not sped
Upon their way! Must we all die?
How many more corpses must lie
To strew Egypt's uncaring earth?
How much are all the living worth?
Are we but sops to Pharaoh's pride?"
Pharaoh accepts the rising tide
Of indignation, he bows to
Necessity. What he must do,
He does. "Bless me, and now be gone
You Israelites! Journey upon
Your way, right now, this very night!
Get out! Depart from Egypt's sight!"

Yahweh has done all He has said.
The Hebrews rise, their steps are sped
To leave Egypt. So hurriedly
They make haste towards the Red Sea.